Maddy McGuire, CEO

Pop-Up Movie Theater

Calico

An Imprint of Magic Wagon
abdopublishing.com

By Emma Bland Smith Illustrated by Lissy Marlin

For my nephews Finn and Ollie Bland, our favorite
movie-and-popcorn pals–EBS

To my lucky stars, thanks for lighting my way–LM

abdopublishing.com

Published by Magic Wagon, a division of ABDO, PO Box 398166,
Minneapolis, Minnesota 55439. Copyright © 2019 by Abdo
Consulting Group, Inc. International copyrights reserved in all
countries. No part of this book may be reproduced in any form
without written permission from the publisher. Calico™ is a
trademark and logo of Magic Wagon.

Printed in the United States of America, North Mankato,
Minnesota.
052018
092018

Written by Emma Bland Smith
Illustrated by Lissy Marlin
Edited by Bridget O'Brien
Art Directed by Laura Mitchell

Library of Congress Control Number: 2018931817

Publisher's Cataloging-in-Publication Data

Names: Smith, Emma Bland, author. | Marlin, Lissy, illustrator.
Title: Pop-up movie theater / by Emma Bland Smith; illustrated by Lissy Marlin.
Description: Minneapolis, Minnesota : Magic Wagon, 2019. | Series: Maddy
McGuire, CEO
Summary: When Maddy's neighbors cancel the annual block party, the budding
    CEO and her best friend, Darcy, hatch a plan to raise funds. A pop-up movie
    theater! But when nobody shows up on movie night, Maddy and Darcy have to
    figure out a new plan.
Identifiers: ISBN 9781532131868 (lib.bdg.) | ISBN 9781532132261 (ebook) |
    ISBN 9781532132469 (Read-to-me ebook)
Subjects: LCSH: Movie theaters--Juvenile fiction. | Fund raising--Juvenile fiction. |
    Block parties--Juvenile fiction. | Children's business enterprises--Juvenile fiction.
Classification: DDC [E]--dc23

TABLE OF CONTENTS

Chapter One

The screen went dark. The lights went on. Maddy sighed, stood up, and stretched.

"That was so good." She looked at her best friend. "Did you like it?"

Darcy was curled up in the seat. She unfolded her legs. "I loved it! Can you believe he found the dog in the boat?"

"I know," said Maddy. She scooted out of the aisle and headed toward the exit. They were the last ones in the theater.

Maddy always liked to stay till the end of the credits. She didn't want to miss anything.

The girls left the dark theater. They blinked in the bright lobby.

The red carpet shone bright. Globe lights encircled posters for upcoming films. The soft sound of popping and the smell of fresh buttered popcorn made everything cozy.

Licking salt off her fingers, she followed Darcy outside. "There's my mom!" Maddy said. Her family's blue car pulled up in front. She and Darcy climbed into the backseat.

"Hi girls," said Mom, smiling over her shoulder as they buckled up. "How was the movie?"

"It was great, but we didn't see Coco or Ava," said Maddy. "They were supposed to be there. That was our plan!"

"Oh, yes," said Mom. She pulled away from the curb and headed toward home. "I saw Coco's dad after I'd dropped you girls off.

"He said he was just too busy and didn't have time to drive them over. I was so sorry. If I'd known, I'd have driven everyone."

"Ohhhh." Driving. The one thing kids couldn't do on their own.

Maddy, Darcy, Coco, and Ava had planned this whole night. They were going to have their parents drop them off at the theater, then watch the movie by themselves! Darn.

Mom turned a corner and drove past the pumpkin patch. It was October 2, and just yesterday the field had filled

up with hundreds of plump orange pumpkins.

And that reminded Maddy of her favorite subject in the whole entire world. "What are you going to be for Halloween, Darcy?" She turned as much as she could in a seat belt.

"A zombie princess!" said Darcy, clapping her hands and grinning. "And Bun-Bun will be my vampire bunny!" Bun-Bun was Darcy's soft, gray rabbit. Maddy loved him.

"Really?" Maddy clapped too, and bounced in her seat. "I'm going to be a zombie pioneer girl! We can be Halloween almost-twins!"

Maddy and Darcy laughed at the coincidence. They were in fourth grade now. None of the girls wanted to be regular princesses and fairies. Scary or gross costumes were much more fun.

The ride ended too soon. Maddy was explaining how she planned to do her white face paint when they arrived at Darcy's house.

Darcy jumped out. Mom continued down the block and around the corner. She pulled into the garage.

Maddy climbed out of the car, thinking about what to use for fake blood. She had some kinks to work out. Good thing she had four weeks to figure it all . . .

"I just remembered!" she said out loud.

"What?" said Mom. Her voice was muffled. She was leaning into the trunk. She'd gone grocery shopping while the girls were at the movie.

"The block party! I'll get to wear my costume at the block party, too. And that's always right before Halloween."

Maddy's neighborhood closed for an all-day block party every October. It was so much fun.

There was a water balloon toss, a barbecue, and a pumpkin carving contest. The kids got to ride their bikes in the street. The local fire truck even visited. They let the kids take pictures manning the steering wheel.

But the best part was the costume parade. The kids kept their costumes a secret until the party. Then they showed up at 11 a.m. on the dot, all dressed up.

People even brought their dogs. Last year, Lucy the poodle wore an orange tutu!

"Mads . . ." said Mom. But Maddy was pounding up the basement stairs. She flung open the door to the kitchen, and ran across the room.

She planted herself in front of the calendar. It hung from its nail on the pantry door. She looked at the space for the next Saturday in October.

Farmers market was written in her mom's scrawl. That was all.

She looked at the next Saturday. *Dentist. Babysit cousins.*

She checked the Sundays, even though the party was always on a Saturday. She saw work deadlines. School PTA meetings. Birthdays of distant relatives.

Nowhere on the calendar, in the whole month of October, was there a mention of the party. Desperate, she even flipped to November. No block party.

Mom hauled the bags of groceries into the kitchen. "Maddy," she began again.

Maddy looked over her shoulder. "Mom, you forgot to write the block party on the calendar."

"Maddy." Mom put down the groceries and looked at her. "There is no block party this year. I'm sorry."

Chapter Two

$160

"What?" Maddy couldn't believe it. Her favorite event of the year, canceled! "No block party? Why?"

"Okay, calm down. I think you'll understand when you hear the reason."

Mom handed Maddy a can of tomatoes. Putting it away in the cupboard, Maddy glanced at the red picture on the label. *Hmm, could work for the fake blood*, she pondered.

"The price went up," continued Mom. She put the turkey bacon into the fridge. "Way up."

"Oh," said Maddy. She understood about things costing too much.

Last summer, she wanted to take horseback riding lessons. But Mom said they were too expensive. So Maddy had raised the money herself.

She organized a summer camp for kids and their pets, called Pet Camp. She'd had to create a budget and keep track of expenses. She'd learned a lot about money.

Mom went on. "You have to get a permit from City Hall to close down the block. It used to be free. But this year the city changed its policy. They raised the prices for things like block party permits."

"How much is it now?"

Mom folded up the empty grocery bags. "One hundred sixty dollars."

One hundred sixty dollars! Maddy plopped down on a stepping stool.

"And there's one more thing," said Mom. "Margaret, Brian, and Monika usually plan the party. They didn't have time to knock on doors, or pass out flyers, asking for donations.

"So we decided to skip the party this year. I know you like it, sweetie. But we'll find other fun things to do."

Maddy nibbled on her pinkie fingernail. One hundred sixty dollars. She started to walk in a slow circle around the kitchen.

"Mom?" she said. She stopped at the counter and clicked on the electric tea kettle. She and Mom had tea together before dinner. It was a tradition they'd started during Pet Camp.

"Uh-huh?" said Mom, looking at the teacup shelf. Maddy pointed to the one with green polka dots. Mom chose a cup with pink flowers on the inside. She set them both on a tray.

"Let me raise the money! I know I can do it. Remember Pet Camp?"

Mom stopped rummaging through the tea bag jar. First she was silent. Then, her voice was slow and even.

"Maddy, this is a bigger deal than taking lessons. It affects an entire block of people. It would be unfair to start, then give up. People would be disappointed."

"But I wouldn't give up! I know I can handle it," said Maddy.

Mom smiled at her. "Actually, I'm pretty sure you could handle it. The other problem is that it's too late to organize something for October. We'd have to reschedule for spring."

"No," said Maddy. "It has to be October! We always have the costume parade!" They couldn't have a block party without a costume parade.

Mom dropped the calendar pages down. "Maddy, I really don't think this is a good idea."

"Not having the most important event of the whole entire year is what's not a good idea. I can do it!" said Maddy.

The tea kettle dinged. Maddy whispered a silent plea. Mom looked at Maddy. She sighed.

Mom poured the hot water into the teapot, and set a few madeleine cookies on a plate. She sat down.

"Okay. Let's pick a date. Then you'd better get to work. You have a lot to do, starting with raising the money for the permit."

Chapter Three

Picking the date for the party was easy. That took five seconds. October 29, the Saturday before Halloween.

Planning the party wasn't going to be hard either. Maddy's block had thrown the party many times. She knew things would pretty much fall into place.

"Brian usually arranges for the fire truck," Mom said. "Stella's parents set up the bouncy house. The Wolf family buys the candy. And the Larsons organize the balloon toss."

Mom made a few calls. Everyone agreed to do their usual job for the party. And whenever people asked, "But what about the permit?"

Mom would answer with, "Maddy's handling it."

"Okay, Mads," said Mom, setting down the phone. "Now it's your turn."

Maddy dipped her madeleine into her now-cold tea and took a bite. She chewed slowly. This was the hard part. How was she going to raise $160?

"I wish I could do another Pet Camp," she said. "But it's not summer."

"Think of something like that. Something you could do at home that people want or need." Mom carried her tea into the living room. "That's called evaluating your market."

Maddy remembered that from last summer. Mom had helped her write a simple business plan.

"The market is the people who are going to buy your product. Your customers," called Mom. "Who is your market, and what do they want?"

Maddy stirred a spoonful of sugar into her tea, quietly, so Mom wouldn't hear. Mom didn't believe in sugar in tea. She took a sip. Mmm.

So, who was her market? The people in the neighborhood. But what did they want? What could she sell them?

Writing it out would help her brainstorm. Maddy reached into her jeans pocket, looking for her small notebook.

She could feel something else in there. She pulled out her movie ticket. It was folded and creased. But it still

made her smile. She set it on the counter and found the notebook.

She wrote *Market: Neighbors.* Then she added *What the market needs is . . .*

Distracted, she let her eyes wander back to the ticket. She giggled. She

thought of the scene where the dog pulled the well-dressed main character off the boat into the water.

She and Darcy had laughed so hard at that part. Coco and Ava would have liked that. Too bad they had missed it.

It really was too bad they didn't have a movie theater on the block. That would be so fun. It would be amazing! It would make theirs the coolest block in . . .

Maddy froze, her eyes wide. That was it! She doodled a ticket, and carefully printed, *Movie Theater.*

Chapter Four

A movie that kids could go to without needing a grown-up to drive them! That was the most absolutely incredible idea for raising money.

She added *Absolutely Incredible* above *Movie Theater.*

Maddy grabbed her notebook. She ran past the living room, where Mom was working on her laptop. She went up the stairs to her room.

It was quiet. Dad and Drew were still out.

She pulled open her art cabinet. Her Pet Camp folder was inside.

There were all the notes she'd taken. It also had a book on basic business skills. She'd found it at a thrift store. At the bottom was the business plan Mom had helped her with.

It was time for a new one.

Maddy found a blank sheet of paper. A business plan helped you figure out what your business was and whether it would be successful.

And this one really needs to be successful! she thought. *What if it's not?*

They wouldn't get the permit. The party would be canceled. And Maddy would disappoint so many people.

She looked back at the business plan for Pet Camp. She read Mom's first question. *What is your idea?*

On the blank page, she wrote: *My idea is a movie theater. We will show movies . . .*

Where? In her room? Too cramped. In the living room? Not very exciting. Outside? Yes!

We will show movies in the backyard.

Luckily, they lived in Northern California. October was usually warm enough to stay outside after dark.

She looked back at the Pet Camp business plan. The next question was *Who are your customers?*

Easy. She'd already answered that downstairs in the kitchen. She wrote *My neighbors.*

Then she added a few notes. *They will want this product because kids can't drive. They will be able to see a movie on our block.*

She looked over her business plan so far. It was very professional. Next question. *How will you spread the word?* Hmm. Maddy decided to skip that one for now.

She read on. The next five questions were about money. The pros called it finances. *What are your start-up costs and expenses? What will you charge per unit?* And on and on.

Maddy crossed her legs and gripped her pencil. Time for math. Ugh. She was terrible at math. How much should she charge?

She looked at the movie ticket again. It was $10.50. Maddy would round to ten dollars even. That was called beating the competitor's price.

We will charge $10 per person, she wrote. She wondered how many people would come.

She counted the kids on the block. Liam and Oliver. Stella and Ike. Alma and Xander. Sylvan and Ingrid. Linus and Owen. Paige, Bea, and Josie.

The teenagers, Miles, Alice, and AJ. Her cousins, Finn, Ollie, Carver, and Aija would come.

She would also invite some of her and Drew's friends. They weren't on the block. But they were still in the neighborhood.

"Let's say 25 people," she said. If 25 people bought tickets at $10, that would make . . . She thought hard for a moment.

"To multiply by ten, just add a zero," she heard her teacher say. Maddy crunched the numbers . . . $250.

But wait! She had forgotten about start-up costs. Two hundred and fifty dollars was only her gross profit.

That was before start-up costs and expenses were taken out. She giggled as she wrote *gross* next to $250. How much money did she need to start with?

She was sure she could borrow a projector from Mr. Morales. He lived up the street. He made them watch slideshows of his family's vacations. So that wouldn't cost anything.

And they could show the movie on a sheet. Her schoolteacher had done that once when the screen broke. Her mom had plenty of white sheets.

But people would want snacks. Popcorn was a must.

And maybe . . . chocolate chip cookies, warm from the oven. Maddy was a pro at making cookies. That would make this better than a real theater.

How much money would she need to buy popcorn? Or the ingredients to make cookies? And maybe some paper bowls and napkins?

She thought $30, just to be safe. *We will need $30 to start with*, she wrote.

She subtracted $30 from $250. Two hundred and twenty dollars. That would be her net profit.

But the permit only cost $160. That left an additional $60. She wondered what to do. Maybe they could rent a photo booth for the party. Or ponies!

But she was getting distracted. *Back on track, Maddy,* she told herself. *You have a lot to handle here!*

She grabbed her painted coffee can and dumped out the contents. A few coins rolled around in a circle before finally settling. Fifty-two cents.

No one was around to witness how broke she was. But Maddy still felt embarrassed. How did this happen?

Oh yeah, she remembered. She'd spent her last few dollars on snacks for Nessie. She was the horse Maddy rode for her lessons.

Where would she get the $30 for her start-up costs? She knew she could borrow from Mom. But she'd done that with Pet Camp.

Getting the money from her parents felt babyish. She wanted this to be like a real business!

Downstairs, the front door clicked open. Footsteps echoed across the hall. Dad was home. Maddy heard her brother Drew's voice.

Would Drew lend her the money? Probably not. He wasn't exactly Mr. Generous when it came to Maddy.

Unless . . . Maddy remembered what Mom had taught her about start-up funds for a business.

A person who lent you money to start a business was called an investor. After you earned your money, you paid back the investor. Plus, sometimes a little extra. The extra was called interest. So the investor could make money, too.

No, Drew wasn't normally Mr. Generous with his sister. If he knew he could make money that might change things.

Maddy jumped up and tore out of her room. She bounded down the stairs. "Dr—" she began.

Her feet went out from under her and she flew through the air. Maddy landed with a loud, painful thump, at the bottom of the stairs.

Chapter Five

"Maddy!" Mom jumped off the couch and ran toward her.

"What was that?" Dad came pounding in from the kitchen.

"Whoa! Are you okay?" Drew asked from the dining room.

Maddy could feel the tears coming. "Ow . . ." Mom helped her up.

This was no time to cry. She was a business woman. She swiped her eyes and pushed her hair back. She knew she would have bruises tomorrow.

But she ignored the aches and pains. Maddy turned to her brother. "Drew, do you want to earn some money?"

"Uh, maybe. I don't know. What do you mean?" said Drew. He was sitting at the dining room table, drawing.

"I'm raising money for the block party permit," Maddy began.

"You mean you're helping Mom do it?" asked Drew.

"No, I'm handling it!" Maddy insisted. Drew raised his eyebrows at her.

"I am!" she said. "Mom, aren't I handling it? You're not even helping me, right?"

Mom nodded. "Yes, you're pretty much on your own. But I'll be here to help if you need it."

Maddy hoped she wouldn't need it. She turned back to Drew. "I'm going to do an outdoor movie to raise the money. But I need money to start with. To buy the snacks and stuff.

"So I need help. Someone to lend me the money, about thirty dollars. And I'd pay you back your money. Plus a little extra, for interest. Will you do it?" Maddy asked.

"Wow, an outdoor movie?" Drew looked up from his drawing. "That's really cool!" Maddy could tell he wished he'd thought of the idea.

"But I need help," said Maddy. "I can't do it without a . . ." She thought for a second, and then said, "an investor. Investors are important."

It worked. Drew nodded. "Yeah, you can borrow $30. I wonder how much interest I'll make on that. Ten percent okay?"

Mom looked up. "Five," she said, raising her eyebrows.

Drew nodded. He started to multiply some numbers on a scratch piece of paper.

Maddy turned to Mom. It was time to put things in motion. "Mom? Can you text Darcy's mom and ask if we can hang out tomorrow?" She ran off to gather supplies.

The next morning, Maddy and Dad walked down the street toward Darcy's house. Maddy explained her plans.

"If I show the movie next weekend, I can get the permit on Monday. Then we'll have two weeks to plan the block party!"

"And Darcy knows all about it?" asked Dad. They started up the front steps of the Lees' building.

"Yeah. I told her about it on the phone yesterday. We're going to be partners."

Maddy didn't get to knock on the door. Darcy opened it and yanked Maddy in. "Come on," she said. "I've got everything set up!"

Darcy sprinted down the hall. Her long black hair swung behind her.

"Bye, Dad," called Maddy.

Darcy had set up a work station in her bedroom. There was a card table with two chairs. A water glass, a clipboard, a notebook, and a pen sat at each spot.

Maddy stared. "Wow," she said. "It's like a real business meeting."

"I know," said Darcy. "I asked my mom what her work meetings are like. And wait, this is the best part!"

She pulled two items off a hook on her door. She handed one to Maddy. "This is a lanyard."

"A lanyard? Like the thing you make at summer camp?"

"No, a different kind. It's what grown-ups wear at conferences."

Darcy put her lanyard on. She showed Maddy the slip at the bottom. She'd inserted a card in each one. Darcy's said, *Darcy Lee, Assistant CEO.*

Maddy's said, *Maddy McGuire, CEO.* A thrill went through her. She was a chief executive officer. The boss!

"But don't you want to be a CEO too? We could be co-CEOs."

"No, I'll be your assistant. I don't know much about business yet."

Maddy joined Darcy at the table. She pulled out a paper in a plastic sleeve. "This is our marketing plan."

"What's marketing?" asked Darcy.

"It's getting people to know about your business," said Maddy. "Like, you know, commercials."

"Ooh, are we going to make a commercial?" asked Darcy.

"I wish," said Maddy. "We're only kids. I think we need to start a little smaller."

Maddy read the plan out loud. "One, make a poster. Put it somewhere where everyone will see it. Two, make flyers. Pass them out to the whole neighborhood."

She paused. "That's it. It's pretty short."

"It's great! I love making posters!" said Darcy. "Did you bring supplies?"

In reply, Maddy tipped open her canvas tote bag. Construction paper, scissors, glitter, stickers, and markers spilled out in a big, colorful mess.

Maddy and Darcy sighed happily.

And got to work.

Chapter Six

Pumpkin, caramel-apple, pecan, or pear? Maddy looked at the pies in the glass case. Her stomach rumbled.

She and Darcy had worked through lunch. Darcy's mom pointed out that it was one o'clock. The girls decided to go out for a business lunch.

They needed to work out a few issues for movie night. Darcy's mom had given them money for pie.

"What will it be, Maddy?" asked Rasheed, the owner.

Maddy felt shy. She'd been to the Pie Place many times before. This was the first time without a grown-up.

But Rasheed was waiting. She looked once more at the selections.

Mom always insisted Maddy get savory pie. Savory, Maddy learned, meant main course-y, not dessert-y.

But today, Mom wasn't here. Today, Maddy was handling things. And she was going sweet!

"A slice of caramel-apple, please," she said.

Darcy ordered pecan and paid. She counted her change and put it in her pocket.

The two girls sat at the long, worn wooden table. Rasheed's wife and co-owner of the bakery, Aliza, brought the slices over.

As they ate, they talked.

"We can't finish the poster and flyers until we decide on a movie. It should be scary, since it's before Halloween," said Maddy.

"Yes, but not too scary!" said Darcy. "Because little kids will be there. We don't want them to cry."

"True." Maddy paused, her fork midair, thinking. They spent a few minutes discussing and finally made a decision. But there were more things to decide on, too.

Where would people sit? On the grass, on blankets.

What if it rained? They'd move to the garage.

When would they get snacks? After school on Friday, with Maddy's mom.

The girls finished their last bites of pie. They brushed the last flakes of pastry off their jeans. The girls felt they had the situation firmly under control. Except for one thing.

"What's the name of the movie theater?" asked Darcy. "The one we go to is called the Empire Theater. We need a name."

"I was thinking the Absolutely Incredible Movie Theater," said Maddy. She felt her cheeks get warm. Was the name too show-offy? But Darcy nodded firmly, approving.

"Bye, girls," called Aliza, as they opened the door.

"By the way," she added. "We'll be having a pop-up pie stand on Halloween. At the corner of 9th Avenue and Irving Street. Be sure to stop by!"

"Okay! Bye!" The girls waved and left the Pie Place. The bell on the big glass door tinkled.

"A pop-up pie stand . . ." said Maddy as they turned up 12th Avenue.

A mom at their school sold flowers in front of the library. She used a red wagon as her stand. She called it a pop-up flower store. Pop-up meant that it was temporary, a one-time thing.

Darcy stopped and grabbed Maddy's arm. She was obviously thinking along the same lines.

"I know!" she said. "The Absolutely Incredible Pop-Up Movie Theater!"

Maddy grinned. "You read my mind!"

Chapter Seven

The rest of the week crept by. The Absolutely Incredible Pop-Up Movie Theater was set to pop up in a few days.

Maddy could barely wait. "Oh, I wish it were Saturday already!" She must have said it at least a million times.

Mom eventually lost her patience. "Mads! I'm going to charge you a dollar every time you say that!" she said.

That did the trick. Maddy was sure Mom was joking. But just in case, she kept her mouth shut. She needed every dollar she had for the movie.

Luckily, she was busy until Saturday. She and Darcy had some jobs to take care of.

On Monday, they tacked the poster on a phone pole.

"Don't you think we should add 'Fund-raiser for block party'?" Darcy looked critically at the poster.

"No," said Maddy. "I want this to be real. Not people donating money to be nice. If people buy tickets because they want to help the party, then it's not a regular business."

And I'm not a CEO, she thought with a frown.

On Tuesday, Maddy printed out flyers from Mom's computer. She paid Mom five cents each, to cover the ink and paper. She dropped a flyer in each mailbox on the block.

On Wednesday, Maddy walked up the street with Mom. They went to borrow the movie projector from Mr. Morales.

On Thursday, Maddy and Darcy stopped at the library after school. They picked up the movie they had put on hold.

On Friday, they used Drew's money to buy snacks. One bag of popcorn kernels, one bag of chocolate chips, butter, paper cups, and napkins. Mom said they could find everything else in the kitchen.

Finally, it was Saturday. Maddy and Darcy struggled with the sheet in the backyard. It was six o'clock. The movie would begin at seven.

Because it was fall, the sun was setting. The light had already started to fade. They needed total darkness for the movie, of course.

"Okay, I've got this corner attached. Now you do yours!" said Maddy.

Just as Darcy secured her corner, Drew came outside. "Did you iron it?"

"What do you mean?" asked Maddy.

"We did this at camp once. If you don't iron the sheet, the movie will be wavy and ripply."

"I didn't know that!" yelled Maddy. She didn't have time for this. She had planned out every minute. And now they'd be behind schedule!

Maddy looked at her brother. She remembered what Mom had taught her about delegating. Delegating was when you asked your team to help.

"Drew, can you do it for me?"

"I was just about to play some basketball," said Drew.

"Drew!" said Maddy. "You are an investor. And you know what, sometimes investors have to help out. Otherwise you might not get your investment back."

Drew paused. He nodded. "Good point. Can I also have a cookie?"

Maddy gave a sigh of relief. "Yes, sure," she said.

Drew took the sheet to the laundry room to iron. The girls ran into the kitchen. They were just in time to hear the oven timer beep.

"Cookies are ready!" said Maddy. She shoved her hand into a pot holder. Darcy opened the oven door.

"Mmm. Smells delicious," said Darcy. She closed her eyes and put her nose in the air. A tantalizing scent of fresh-baked cookies wafted through the room.

The house smelled even better by the time the popcorn had been popped. They drizzled it with melted butter and salt.

The girls organized the snacks into cups and onto trays. They set them on a folding table covered with a red checkered tablecloth. It had a sign marked *Help yourselves!*

It was 6:55. Only five minutes left!

Drew hung the smooth sheet. Darcy and Maddy set up a counter on the sidewalk. People would pay for tickets here. Then they'd walk through the garage to the backyard.

It was 6:58. Maddy looked nervously up and down the almost-dark street. "I thought people would be here by now."

She chewed on her pinkie fingernail. Then she quickly put her hand behind her back.

Darcy jumped up. "Let's do a sound check!" she said. That would help pass the last few minutes anyway. Darcy and Maddy headed to the projector.

Maddy pressed play. Music spilled out. An image appeared on the sheet, somewhat off-center.

"Let me fix it." Darcy fiddled with it until the image was centered.

"Perfect!" said Maddy. "Okay, let's go. There might be a line by now!"

They ran back out to the street. Drew was dribbling his basketball. Mom and Dad sat on the front steps. There was no one else.

"No one's coming!" cried Maddy. "All this work, and it's a total failure!"

"I bet people are just running late," said Mom.

"No," said Maddy, her face growing hot. "No one's coming, I know it!"

"I agree with Maddy," said Drew, unhelpfully. "It's already 7:05. The movie was supposed to start five minutes ago. Usually people get to these things early. They'd want to get a good spot."

Maddy knew Drew was right. She ran inside and threw herself on the couch. She burst into tears.

Chapter Eight

Maddy heaved big sobs. She couldn't believe no one had showed up for the movie!

The couch shifted as someone sat down beside her. It was Darcy.

Maddy wiped her face and sat up. It was nice of Darcy to come in and comfort her. "It's not that bad," she said.

"Yes, it is," said Maddy, putting her arms around her knees.

"Think about it. You're planning a party. You ask someone, 'How could this go wrong? What is the worst, I mean the worst thing that could possibly happen?'

"They would answer, 'No one showing up.' And that's what just happened! I feel like this is a scene from a dumb TV show!"

Except that this was real life. And there wasn't going to be any happy ending.

Her movie was a flop. And now she wouldn't be able to get the permit.

She'd have to tell everyone there wouldn't be a block party after all!

Plus she wouldn't be able to pay Drew back his thirty dollars! Why did she ever think she could handle something this important?

Dad poked his head around the door frame. "Mads, why don't you get a cider at the Pie Place? My treat. We'll clean up here."

Maddy nodded and wiped the last tears off her face. "Okay. Thanks."

She and Darcy walked down the street. They passed some neighbor kids making chalk drawings on the sidewalk. Why hadn't they come to the movie?

She couldn't bring herself to ask. But Darcy could. "Why didn't you guys come to our pop-up movie?"

Stella stopped drawing her chalk rainbow. She looked up nervously. "My mom thought it was expensive."

Linus chimed in. "Why do you need all that money, anyway?" he asked. "It's sort of greedy!"

Maddy's cheeks burned. She started to run.

Could things get any worse? Now everyone thought she was greedy!

"Maddy," panted Darcy, catching up. "Just tell them it's for a good cause! The money's not for you. You're the opposite of greedy."

"But then they'll think I'm not a real business person."

"But..." said Darcy. They had arrived at the Pie Place. Maddy opened the door and the bell tinkled.

"Hi girls," said Aliza, looking up from slicing an apple pie. "Oh, Maddy, what's wrong? Are you crying?"

Maddy shook her head. "It's okay. We're just having a problem with our pop-up movie theater."

"Oh, I'm sorry," said Aliza.

Rasheed came out of the kitchen. He took a look at Maddy and Darcy.

"Hard day?" he asked. "Hot apple ciders on me."

"Oh, we can pay." Maddy held up her ten dollars.

"Nope, this is a gift," Rasheed said.

"Thank you," said Maddy. Then she whispered to Darcy. "Let's use the money to buy some pie, instead."

"Okay." The girls discussed their options while Rasheed stirred spices into the ciders. He even stuck in cinnamon sticks.

"We'll also take two slices of pumpkin pie," said Darcy.

As Maddy paid, she looked at the prices over the counter. The apple ciders were two dollars each. The slices of pie were three.

She quickly added the numbers in her head. They had planned to spend four dollars, but had spent six. That was two dollars more than they had intended to.

Huh, Maddy thought. *Maybe I'm not that bad at math after all.*

Maddy knew Rasheed had not expected the girls to buy pie. He had only meant to do a nice thing.

By giving them something for free, he had unintentionally encouraged them to buy something else. His kindness had paid off for him.

Maddy took her first sip. And just like that, she knew what to do. She could fix this movie disaster.

Chapter Nine

Maddy liked sitting at the worn wooden table. She liked listening to the classical music Rasheed and Aliza always played. But Maddy knew she had no time to spare.

"Can we take our pie to go, please?" she asked. Aliza wrapped the slices and slipped them into paper bags.

The girls finished their ciders, said goodbyes, and ran out onto the sidewalk. The bell on the door tinkled behind them.

Maddy explained everything as she and Darcy ran up the street. Darcy jumped up and down. "I'll change the poster, and you work on a flyer."

"Can we go to your house?" asked Maddy. All the art supplies were still at Darcy's.

The girls stopped at Maddy's first. Maddy told her parents and Drew about the new plan.

"Mads, are you sure you want to try this again?" Mom asked.

"And if you're rescheduling it for tomorrow," said Dad, "that's not giving a lot of notice. You'll feel even worse if it doesn't work."

Maddy said nothing. She had been so sure a minute ago. But then, she had been sure of her last plan, too.

Drew sat at the kitchen counter. He was reading and munching on a cookie. One of Maddy's fresh-baked cookies. And from the crumbs on the counter, it wasn't his first.

"It'll work," he said. "Because these chocolate chip cookies are delicious."

He looked up briefly, then went back to his book.

Maddy smiled. "It'll work."

"I think you're right," said Dad. "But there is one issue. You might need to make more cookies." He looked at the half-eaten one in his hand.

"And the popcorn will be stale by tomorrow," said Darcy. "We'll have to make more. And we'll need more money for that."

Maddy didn't miss a beat. "That's what I'll use the extra money for!" she cried. She clapped her hands.

"Great idea, Mads," said Mom. "That sixty dollars was your cushion. For emergencies like this one."

"And you only need thirty dollars," said Darcy. "So you'll still have extra leftover for the party."

Maddy hesitated. "But I don't have the extra thirty dollars yet . . ."

Mom jumped up. "I'm going to lend it to you. No arguing! I'll take . . . a dozen cookies as interest!"

A warm feeling bubbled up inside Maddy. She looked around at her family and smiled. "Thanks," she said.

Maddy and Darcy walked up the steps to Darcy's building. They knocked on the left-side door. The right-side door was the apartment where Darcy's grandmother lived.

They called her Poh-Poh, which meant "grandma" in Chinese. There were always yummy smells coming from under her door. Things like homemade dumplings and garlic-sautéed vegetables.

Today, Maddy smelled chicken chow mein. Her stomach rumbled and she remembered the pie they carried.

"We can handle this," she said to Darcy. "But first, let's eat. Do you think Poh-Poh would invite us over for dinner? I feel like something savory before my pie."

Chapter Ten

It was 6:30 p.m. on Sunday. Maddy had a case of the nerves. Her dad was right. If no one showed up, she'd feel even worse than before.

And what did Drew know? He thought all cookies were delicious.

She finished ironing the sheet and held it up. There was a tiny crease. She flopped it back down on the ironing board. It had to be perfect!

Mom popped in the laundry room. "What are you doing, Mads?"

"Anything to distract myself!" said Maddy, pressing the iron harder. She lifted it, and smiled to see the smooth white sheet underneath. Ironing was magical.

"Here," said Mom. "I'll hang that. Why don't you just go read or listen to an audiobook until seven? Everything else is ready."

Maddy was sure she would not be able to concentrate. "No, I think I'd better make more popcorn!"

"Really?" said Mom. "You already have enough to feed an army."

But Maddy was skidding down the hall to the kitchen. She reached for pots, jars, and bowls.

She turned on the burner, poured oil in the pot, and dropped in a cup of kernels. She waited. She drummed her fingers on the counter. Then she put her hair up in a ponytail.

She turned on the radio to help pass the time, setting the volume loud. She zoned out, focused on cooking and prepping.

"Maddy!" She jumped. Who was calling her?

How much time had passed? The clock blinked 6:45 p.m.

Mom stepped into the room. Her hands covered her ears. Maddy quickly turned down the volume. But the room was not instantly quiet.

"What's all that noise?" she asked her mom. "Are you watching TV?"

"It's the guests!" said Mom. "Your plan worked. There's a line outside."

Maddy stood for just a moment, her mouth open, her heart racing.

Then she raced down the stairs and out the front door.

There was Coco and Ava. And all the neighbor kids. And all of Maddy's cousins.

There was Mr. Morales. And Ms. Kelly, the dance teacher who lived across the street. Even Rasheed and Aliza from the Pie Place.

When Maddy looked up the block, she saw more people. Maya was leading her younger sister Antonia with one hand. She carried a blanket in the other.

Drew's best friend Will was on his bike. He lived a whole ten blocks away! More bikes and a few strollers were parked in front of the house.

Maddy's stomach flopped. *I can handle this*, she said to herself. She adjusted her event staff name tag and took a deep breath.

She said, "Please walk through here to the backyard. The movie will begin in fifteen minutes."

The group followed her. "It's so cool how you're offering the movie for free," said Will.

"Thanks," said Maddy.

"And since the movie is free, I have money for snacks!" Will headed to the table with the checkered cloth. A sign, in Darcy's neat handwriting, read *Cookies: $2. Popcorn: $3.*

Will pointed. "I'll take two of each," he said.

Maddy slipped behind the table and opened her cash box. She did the math in her head. "That'll be ten dollars," she said.

Will walked away and grabbed a spot on the grass.

Ms. Kelly stepped up. She had her three nieces and nephews with her. She bought one of everything for them. Behind her, the line grew.

Darcy came running in. Maddy beckoned frantically to her. Everyone clamored for snacks. "Darcy, help me!"

With two people behind the table, things went faster. Soon everyone was settled on the grass with their treats.

Drew called to her. "Should I press play?" He waited by the projector.

"Wait," said Darcy. She ran over and stepped in front of the crowd.

What was Darcy doing?

"Attention, please," called Darcy, and the crowd quieted down. "Thank you for coming, and for buying so many snacks!

"All the profits are paying for this year's block party permit. It was Maddy's idea. If it weren't for her, there wouldn't be a party this year!"

The crowd was quiet. Maddy's cheeks burned. What were people thinking?

And then the applause and cheers rang out. Maddy couldn't keep the grin off her face.

The sky faded to black. The lights Dad had strung across the yard twinkled. The movie finally began. Maddy closed the cash box and ran into the house.

Mom was in the kitchen.

"Mom, it worked!" said Maddy. "Even more people than I expected came. I never thought I would earn more money by making the movie free."

"It was a brilliant plan," said Mom, smiling. "My grandmother used to say, 'You catch more flies with honey than with vinegar.' "

Maddy considered that. "I like honey," she said. "But I think chocolate chip cookies make a better trap." She ran to claim her spot next to Darcy on their blanket.

Two weeks later, Maddy and Darcy got ready for the costume parade. They looked in Maddy's mirror.

"Wow, you are one creepy zombie pioneer girl!" said Darcy.

"And you look really pretty and scary!" said Maddy.

Maddy wore her flower-printed bonnet from last Halloween's costume.

She'd been a regular pioneer girl. It was now ripped and stained.

Darcy's black zombie princess dress puffed out. Maddy wondered if she was going to have trouble getting through the door.

They looked awesome.

Suddenly, a blast of music floated in through the window. "The Monster Mash!" The costume parade was about to start!

Darcy scooped up Bun-Bun. He wore a black cape with a high collar. The girls raced out of the house.

The pumpkin-carving station was under a tree. Water balloon buckets sat waiting for their big moment. Picnic tables lined the street, ready for the barbecue. Platters of candy beckoned.

Everything was perfect. Maddy's heart raced with excitement.

The girls headed toward where the kids and dogs lined up for the parade. Someone tapped Maddy on the shoulder.

It was Drew. "Some grown-up gave this to me for you," he said. He handed her an envelope.

She opened it and took out a card. The front had a drawing of a movie theater on it. Inside were dozens of signatures. Even the littlest kids had scrawled their names.

A note was printed in the middle. *Thank you for saving the block party, Maddy! You're a top-notch CEO!*

She smiled, hitched up her ripped skirt, and got in the parade line.

A GUIDE FOR KID ENTREPRENEURS
Part 2: Seek Investors

When you start a business, you'll usually have start-up costs and expenses. If your piggy bank is empty, you may need to borrow from an investor. An investor is often paid back their loan, plus interest.

Use the following formula to calculate how much you'll owe:

1. Amount borrowed x interest rate = interest

2. Amount borrowed + interest = amount owed

Example:

1. $30 x 0.05 = $1.50

2. $30 + $1.50 = $31.50.

You must pay your investor $31.50.

AUTHOR BIOGRAPHY

Like her character Maddy McGuire, Emma Bland Smith loves coming up with crazy schemes, and writing children's books is her favorite one yet. Her first book was the award-winning Journey: Based on the True Story of OR7, the Most Famous Wolf in the West. Emma also works as a librarian in San Francisco, where she lives with her husband and two kids. (She hopes her neighbors will recognize the setting of the Maddy McGuire series!) Visit emmabsmith.com to learn more about Emma and her other books.

ILLUSTRATOR BIOGRAPHY

Lissy is an illustrator with a passion and love for animation, visual development, and children's books. She was born and raised in the Dominican Republic before moving to the United States, where she studied illustration at the University of the Arts of Philadelphia. Her passion with illustration and animation truly began after watching Spirited Away. Since then, Hayao Miyazaki has been her biggest artistic influence, while making people smile with beautiful and inspiring images has been her main purpose as an artist. Lissy absolutely loves collecting art books of all kinds, stargazing, traveling, and learning about different languages and cultures.